Text © Beth Shoshan 2006
Illustrations © Jacqueline East 2006
The right of Jacqueline East to be identified
as the illustrator of this work has been
asserted by her in accordance with the Copyright,
Designs and Patents Act, 1988

This edition published by Parragon in 2007
Parragon, Queen Street House, 4 Queen Street, Bath, BA1 1HE, UK
Published by arrangement with Meadowside Children's Books,
185 Fleet Street, London, EC4A 2HS.

A CIP catalogue record for this book
is available from the British Library
Printed in China

ISBN 978-1-4054-9535-6

Cuddle!

Written by
Beth Shoshan

Illustrated by
Jacqueline East

PaRRagon

Bath · New York · Singapore · Hong Kong · Cologne · Delhi · Melbourne

I'd cuddle a whale,
but I might be
too small,

I'd cuddle
a giraffe,
but I think
he's too tall.

I'd cuddle
a hedgehog
but, ouch!
they're so spiky,

I'd cuddle a crocodile.

If I cuddled
a gorilla

I would end up
much thinner,

If I cuddled a tiger
I'd end up as dinner.

I'd cuddle a skunk
but I think they're
too smelly,

I'd cuddle a shark

but I'd be in his belly!

I'd cuddle
a python

way up high
in a tree,

I'd cuddle
a hippo
who might just
squash me.

I'd cuddle a lion

but he'd bite off my head,

Do you think
I can cuddle
my teddy bear
instead?

For Uncle John
&
Aunty Sheila

J.E.